PEANUTS®

Time for School, CHARLIE BROWN

by Charles M. Schulz

adapted by Maggie Testa

illustrated by Robert Pope

Ready-to-Read

Simon Spotlight
New York   London   Toronto   Sydney   New Delhi

SIMON SPOTLIGHT
An imprint of Simon & Schuster Children's Publishing Division
1230 Avenue of the Americas, New York, New York 10020
This Simon Spotlight edition May 2015
© 2015 Peanuts Worldwide LLC

For information about special discounts for bulk purchases, please contact Simon & Schuster Special Sales at
1-866-506-1949 or business@simonandschuster.com.
The Simon and Schuster Speakers Bureau can bring authors to your live event. For more information
or to book an event contact the Simon and Schuster Speakers Bureau at 1-866-248-3049 or visit our website at
www.simonspeakers.com
Manufactured in the United States of America 0315 LAK
2 4 6 8 10 9 7 5 3 1
ISBN 978-1-4814-3606-9 (hc)
ISBN 978-1-4814-3605-2 (pbk)
ISBN 978-1-4814-3607-6 (eBook)

Poor Charlie Brown!
He can't kick a football.
Or throw a decent pitch.
Or even fly a kite.
But when it comes to
worrying about school,
he is the world champ!

"You look down, Charlie Brown,"
Linus says.

"I worry about school a lot,"
Charlie Brown replies.
"And then I worry about worrying
so much about school!"

Charlie Brown decides to get help.
"What's your problem?" Lucy asks.
"I worry about tomorrow."
Charlie Brown answers.
"Then when tomorrow becomes
today, I start worrying about
tomorrow again!"

"I think I can help you,"
Lucy tells Charlie Brown.
"What you need is confidence!"

"Throw out your chest
and face the future!" Lucy shouts.
"Now raise your arm
and clench your fist!"
Charlie Brown does what
Lucy tells him to do.
Suddenly Charlie Brown isn't
worried about school anymore!

He might ace every pop quiz!
He might become hall monitor!
He might even talk to the
Little Red-Haired Girl!
Lucy interrupts Charlie Brown's
daydream.
"You look ridiculous!" she says.

A few days after school starts, the teacher tells the students about the spelling bee.

Charlie Brown thinks
about entering it.
It could be good for him.
He could gain confidence.

Charlie Brown goes to raise his
hand to volunteer.
But his hand won't go up.
"My hand is smarter than I am,"
Charlie Brown groans.

Charlie Brown enters
the spelling bee anyway.
"You're crazy," Lucy whispers.
"Don't do it.
You'll just make a fool of yourself!"

Charlie Brown throws his hands
up in the air.
"I can try, can't I?"
Charlie Brown asks.

"What's the good of living if you don't try a few things?"

Lucy leans over again.
"Spell 'Acetylholinesterase'!"
Charlie Brown gulps.

"Maybe I shouldn't have entered," he says.

But as the spelling bee
gets closer and closer,
Charlie Brown gets braver.
He feels more confident.
"Nobody thinks I can win, Snoopy,"
Charlie Brown tells his dog.
"But I'm going to show them."

"I do have trouble remembering some rules," Charlie Brown admits. "'I' before 'B' except after 'T'? Is it 'V' before 'Z' except after 'E'?" *Good grief,* thinks Snoopy!

It is the day of the spelling bee.
Charlie Brown feels calm.
He feels confident.

All the words in the first round
are easy, he thinks.

Soon it is Charlie Brown's turn.
"Maze?" he repeats
after the teacher gives him the
word.

Charlie Brown isn't worried.
He smiles. He takes a deep breath.
He begins to spell.
"M-A-Y-S!"

Charlie Brown blows it!
Soon he is back at his desk and he
is worrying.
What will his friends say?
What will Snoopy do?

"Yes, ma'am?" Charlie Brown answers when his teacher calls his name.
"Why did I have my head on my desk?"

"Because I blew the spelling bee!"
Charlie Brown yells.
"That's why!"
Charlie Brown covers his mouth
with his hands.
Yelling at the teacher is
never a good idea!

"Oh, good grief!" he says.
It is the worst day
of Charlie Brown's life.
He woke up looking forward
to the spelling bee.
And he ended up
in the principal's office.

"On a day like this, a person
really needs his faithful dog
to come running out to greet him!"
Charlie Brown says on his walk
home.

Snoopy is there waiting for Charlie
Brown when he gets home.

Happiness is a warm puppy.

Poor Charlie Brown!
He can't kick a football.
Or throw a decent pitch.
Or even fly a kite.
But at least he has Snoopy!

Charlie Brown is never happier than when he's with Snoopy.
"What a pair!" Lucy says.